Phonics Friends

Ben, Billy, and the Birdhouse
The Sound of **B**

The
**Child's
World**

By Cecilia Minden and Joanne Meier

The Child's World

Published in the United States of America
by The Child's World®
PO Box 326
Chanhassen, MN 55317-0326
800-599-READ
www.childsworld.com

*A special thank you to Tony Schiller for accepting the role
of "Uncle Bob."*

The Child's World®: Mary Berendes, Publishing Director

Editorial Directions, Inc.: E. Russell Primm, Editorial
Director and Project Editor; Katie Marsico, Associate
Editor; Judith Shiffer, Associate Editor and School Media
Specialist; Linda S. Koutris, Photo Researcher and
Selector

The Design Lab: Kathleen Petelinsek, Design and Page
Production

Photographs ©: Photo setting and photography by
Romie and Alice Flanagan/Flanagan Publishing
Services: 6, 8, 10, 14, 16, 20; Corbis: cover, 4;
Getty Images/Photodisc Blue: 12, 18.

Library of Congress Cataloging-in-Publication Data
Minden, Cecilia.
  Ben, Billy, and the birdhouse : the sound of B /
by Cecilia Minden and Joanne Meier.
    p. cm. — (Phonics friends)
  Summary: Simple text, featuring the consonant B,
describes how Ben, Billy, and Uncle Bob build a
birdhouse.
  ISBN 1-59296-289-0 (library bound : alk. paper)
  [1. English language—Phonetics. 2. Reading.] I. Meier,
Joanne D. II. Title. III. Series.
  PZ7.M6539Be 2004
  [E]—dc22
                                    2004001700

Note to parents and educators:

The Child's World® has created Phonics Friends with the goal of exposing children to engaging stories and pictures that assist in phonics development. The books in the series will help children learn the relationships between the letters of written language and the individual sounds of spoken language. This contact helps children learn to use these relationships to read and write words.

The books in this series follow a similar format. An introductory page, to be read by an adult, introduces the child to the phonics feature, or sound, that will be highlighted in the book. Read this page to the child, stressing the phonic feature. Help the student learn how to form the sound with her mouth. The Phonics Friends story and engaging photographs follow the introduction. At the end of the story, word lists categorize the feature words into their phonic element. Additional information on using these lists is on The Child's World® Web site listed at the top of this page.

Each book in this series has been carefully written to meet specific readability requirements. Close attention has been paid to elements such as word count, sentence length, and vocabulary. Readability formulas measure the ease with which the text can be read and understood. Each Phonics Friends book has been analyzed using the Spache readability formula. For more information on this formula, as well as the levels for each of the books in this series please visit The Child's World® Web site.

Reading research suggests that systematic phonics instruction can greatly improve students' word recognition, spelling, and comprehension skills. The Phonics Friends series assists in the teaching of phonics by providing students with important opportunities to apply their knowledge of phonics as they read words, sentences, and text.

This is the letter *b*.

In this book, you will read words that have the *b* sound as in:

bird, box, bag, and *ball.*

I am Ben.

This is my best friend, Billy.

Billy is also my brother!

This is our Uncle Bob.

We are building a house

for a bird.

Here is a box of wood.

We will need wood.

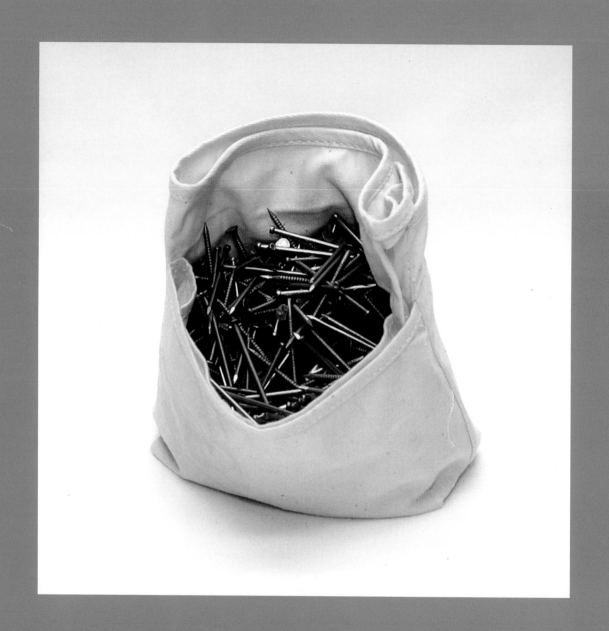

Here is a bag of nails.

We will need nails.

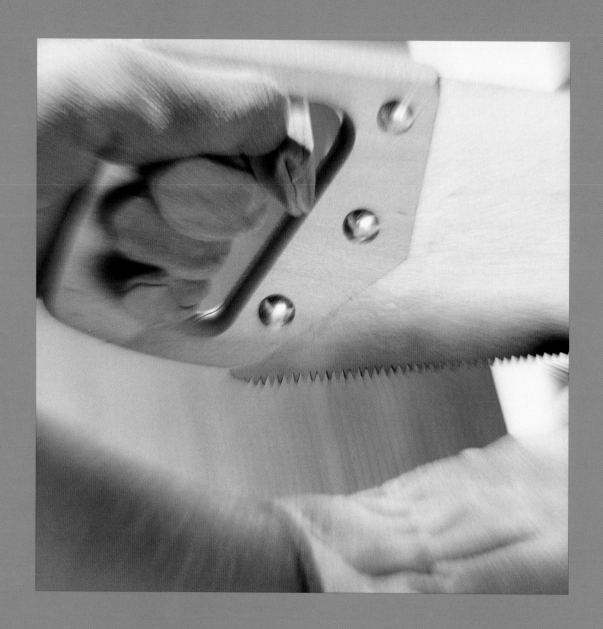

Uncle Bob cuts the wood.

The boys build the house.

It is a beautiful house.

They paint it bright blue.

Uncle Bob finds a branch.

He hangs up the house.

"Someday I will build houses.

The houses will be big," says Ben.

"Someday I will build parks.

Children can play ball," says Billy.

"Look," says Uncle Bob.

"A bird is in the house!"

Fun Facts

Not all birds will make their nests in birdhouses. Owls, woodpeckers, chickadees, wrens, bluebirds, starlings, martins, sparrows, and finches are some that do. Other birds, however, prefer to live in groups. As a result, some people build birdhouses that resemble miniature apartment buildings. These birdhouses have more than one level and can house more than 20 birds!

If you like building things, imagine helping build the Petronas Twin Towers in Malaysia. Many people consider this to be the tallest building in the world! The Sears Tower in Chicago, Illinois, is the tallest building in the United States.

Activity

Building Your Own Birdhouse

With the help of a parent or other adult, you can build your own birdhouse! First, decide what kind of bird you are building the house for. This will affect the size and shape of the house, as well as the materials you use to build it. Once you have finished the birdhouse, pick a good place to put your birdhouse. Many people say the best spot is near a tree or bush. Once the birdhouse is built, keep a journal describing the bird or birds that move in.

To Learn More

Books
About the Sound of B
Flanagan, Alice K. *I Like Bugs: The Sound of B*. Chanhassen, Minn.: The
    Child's World, 2000.

About Best Friends
Parr, Todd. *The Best Friends Book*. Boston: Little, Brown, 2000.
Snyder, Margaret, Ron Rodecker, and Bob Berry (illustrator). *Best Friends*.
    New York: Random House, 2001.

About Birdhouses
Haus, Robyn, and Stan Jaskiel (illustrator). *Make Your Own Birdhouses and
    Feeders*. Charlotte, Vt.: Williamson Publishing, 2001.
Ziefert, Harriet, and Donald Dreifuss (illustrator). *Birdhouse for Rent*. Boston:
    Houghton Mifflin, 2001.

About Building Things
Hayward, Linda. *A Day in the Life of a Builder*. New York: Dorling Kindersley,
    2001.
Tarsky, Sue, and Alex Ayliffe (illustrator). *The Busy Building Book*. New York:
    G. P. Putnam, 1998.

Web Sites
Visit our home page for lots of links about the Sound of B:
http://www.childsworld.com/links.html

Note to Parents, Teachers, and Librarians: We routinely check our Web links to make
sure they're safe, active sites—so encourage your readers to check them out!

B Feature Words

Proper Names
Ben
Billy
Bob

Feature Words in Initial Position
bag
ball
beautiful
best
big
bird
box
boy
build
building

Feature Words with Blends
blue
branch
bright
brother

About the Authors

Cecilia Minden, PhD, directs the Language and Literacy Program at the Harvard Graduate School of Education. She is a reading specialist with classroom and administrative experience in grades K–12. She earned her PhD in reading education from the University of Virginia. Cecilia and her husband Dave Cupp enjoy sharing their love of reading with their granddaughter Chelsea.

Joanne Meier, PhD, has worked as an elementary school teacher and university professor. She earned her BA in early childhood education from the University of South Carolina, and her MEd and PhD in education from the University of Virginia. She currently works as a literacy consultant for schools and private organizations. Joanne Meier lives with her husband Eric, and spends most of her time chasing her two daughters, Kella and Erin, and her two cats, Sam and Gilly, in Charlottesville, Virginia.